MIGHTY READER

MAKES THE GRADE

Will Hillenbrand

HOLIDAY HOUSE · NEW YORK

To Jane, a Mighty Partner

HOLIDAY HOUSE is registered in the U.S. Patent and Trademark Office
Printed and bound in June 2021 at Toppan Leefung, Dong Guan City, China.
This artwork was created digitally with Adobe Fresco.
www.holidayhouse.com
First Edition
1 3 5 7 9 10 8 6 4 2

Library of Congress Cataloging-in-Publication Data

Names: Hillenbrand, Will, author, illustrator.
Title: Mighty Reader makes the grade / Will Hillenbrand.
Description: First edition. | New York : Holiday House, [2021] | Audience:
Ages 4-8. | Audience: Grades K-1. | Summary: "Mighty Reader helps
classmate Lulu overcome test anxiety using reading strategies"—Provided by publisher.
Identifiers: LCCN 2020050862 | ISBN 9780823444991 (hardcover)
Subjects: CYAC: Test anxiety—Fiction. | Reading—Fiction.
Superheroes—Fiction. | Dogs—Fiction. | Schools—Fiction.
Classification: LCC PZ7.H55773 Mm 2021 | DDC [E]—dc23
LC record available at https://lccn.loc.gov/2020050862
ISBN: 978-0-8234-4499-1 (hardcover)

Lulu stumbled.

Ouch!

Where am I?

Standard Street

Test Avenue

What in the world?

BUS STOP
NO SERVICE TODAY

What . . . ?

Got to block that evil-eye thing.

Run . . . hide!

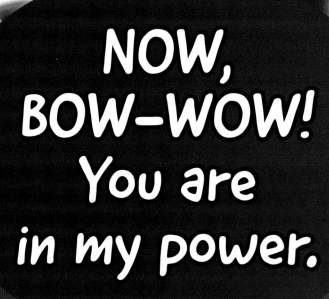

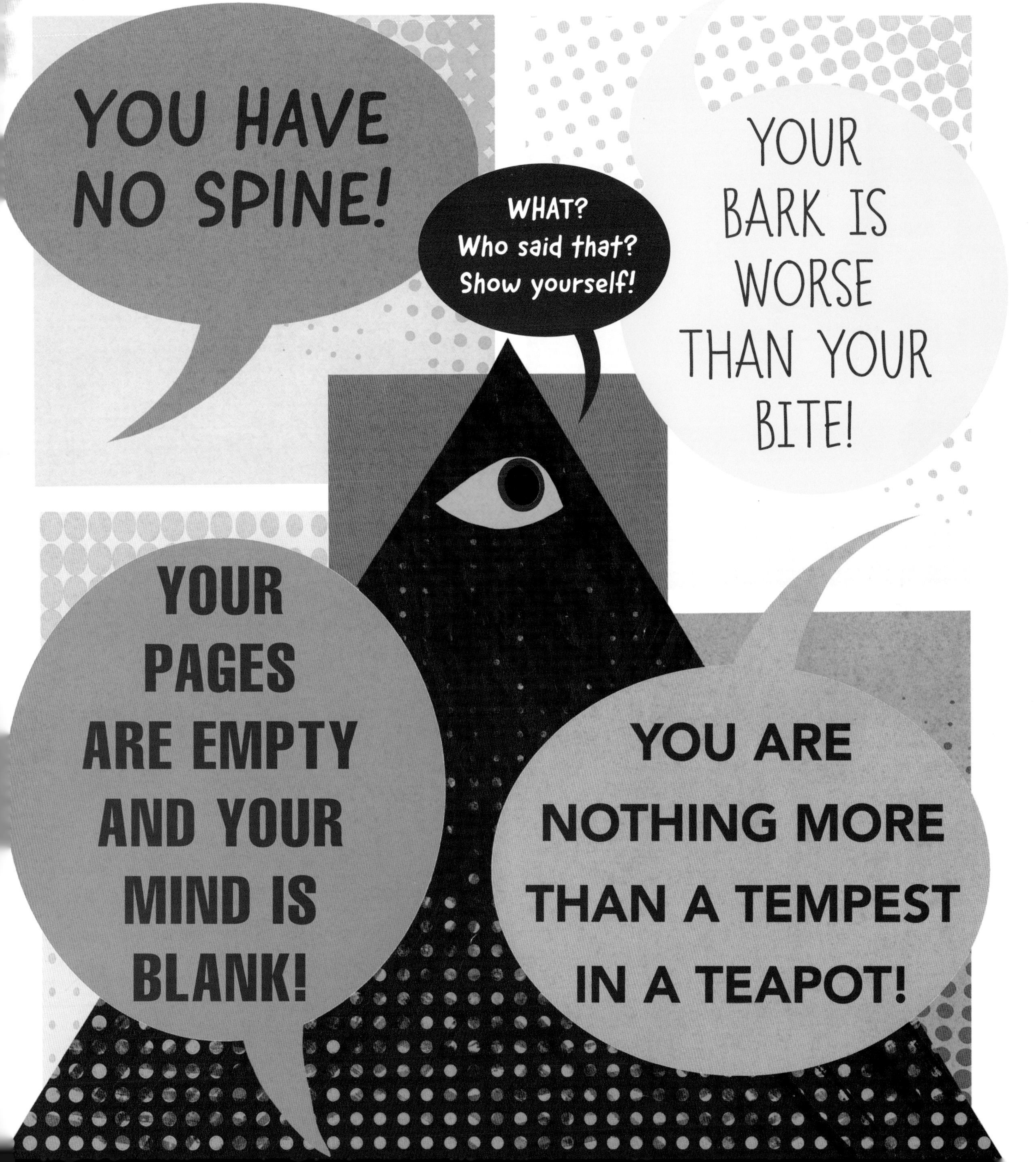
YOU HAVE NO SPINE!
WHAT? Who said that? Show yourself!
YOUR BARK IS WORSE THAN YOUR BITE!
YOUR PAGES ARE EMPTY AND YOUR MIND IS BLANK!
YOU ARE NOTHING MORE THAN A TEMPEST IN A TEAPOT!

Barkley and Hugo choose blocks, and Lulu chooses the library.

Looks like the therapy has relaxed Lulu a little too much.

Z

I'll fix that.

Peek-a-boo, I see Lulu!

I knew IT would be back! AACKKKKK!

Fortunately, Hugo knew just what to do.

DRESS-UP CENTER

Mighty Reader scanned the backpacks with his X-ray vision. He found Lulu's T-shirt . . .

. . . but would he be too late?

PARTNER POWER

Slow Down and Listen

Read the Whole Book

The test begins. Tick-tock, tick-tock.